Hey Jack!

Hey Jack! Books

First American Edition 2023
Kane Miller, A Division of EDC Publishing

Text copyright © 2022 Sally Rippin
Illustration copyright © 2022 Stephanie Spartels
Series design copyright © 2023 Hardie Grant Children's Publishing
Original Title: Hey Jack!: *The Special Guest*
First published in Australia by Hardie Grant Children's Publishing

Kane Miller, A Division of EDC Publishing
5402 S 122nd E Ave
Tulsa, OK 74146
www.kanemiller.com

Library of Congress Control Number: 2022945287
Printed and bound in the United States of America
1 2 3 4 5 6 7 8 9 10

ISBN: 978-1-68464-667-8

The Special Guest

By Sally Rippin

Illustrated by Stephanie Spartels

Kane Miller

A DIVISION OF EDC PUBLISHING

Chapter One

This is Jack. Today Jack is in a happy mood. "It's my turn for Mr. Egg!" he tells Billie.

"That's so exciting!" says Billie. Billie is Jack's best friend. She lives next door. They walk to school together every day.

Today, both of them **run** ahead of Jack's dad. They can't wait to get to school.

When Jack and Billie
reach their classroom,
Jack runs inside to give
Mr. Egg a hug. Mr. Egg
is the class toy.

Everyone gets to take
Mr. Egg home for a
weekend. They have to
look after him. They
take him everywhere
and take photos of him.
The photos go into a
big book. The book is
very **funny**.

4

At the end of the day the bell rings. Everyone in Jack's class stands up to go home.

"Hold on," says Ms. Walton. "Whose turn is it to take Mr. Egg this weekend?"

"Mine!" says Jack.

Ms. Walton smiles. She hands the toy to Jack.

"Great, Jack! I'm sure Mr. Egg will have some fun **adventures** at your house."

That night, Jack puts Mr. Egg to bed. "We are going to have the best weekend!" he tells him. Mr. Egg looks happy.

The next morning, Jack looks at his list of things to do. He has lots of exciting things planned. First, he and Mr. Egg put on helmets and go skateboarding with Scraps, Jack's dog.

Next, Jack and his parents have yum cha for lunch. Mr. Egg loves the dumplings!

In the afternoon, Jack and Mr. Egg play soccer. They play against Scraps and Billie. Mr. Egg is a great goalkeeper.

"Tomorrow we are going on a hike," Jack tells Mr. Egg at bedtime. He snuggles down to sleep.

"Billie and Scraps are coming, too. It's going to be so cool!"

But the next morning when Jack wakes, Mr. Egg has **gone!**

Chapter Two

Jack jumps out of bed.

His heart begins to **race**.

Where is Mr. Egg? Jack

looks under the bed. He

peeks behind the curtains.

Where could Mr. Egg be?

Jack feels **worried**. What if he can't find him before school on Monday?

Jack needs **help**. And fast! He gets dressed, then runs outside to find Billie. Jack squeezes through the hole in their fence. Then he runs up to her back door and knocks loudly.

"Hey, Jack!" says Billie. "I'm just finishing my breakfast."

"I need to talk to you," Jack whispers. He grabs Billie's hand. They run down to the shed at the end of her backyard.

"Something **terrible** has happened!" Jack tells Billie. His voice sounds squeaky and **scared**.

"What?" says Billie.

"Mr. Egg is missing!"

Jack says.

Billie frowns. "What?" she

says. "That's impossible!"

"It's true!" Jack says. "He was on my bed last night. Now he's gone!"

"Have you told your mom and dad?" says Billie.

"No!" says Jack. "I can't tell them. They might tell Ms. Walton. Then she will be **mad** at me!"

They hear Jack's dad calling from over the fence. "Jack! We are going soon. Come and have some breakfast."

"What are we going
to do about today?"
Billie says. "Mr. Egg was
supposed to come on
our **hike**."

"I know," says Jack. "I'll
have to tell Mom and
Dad we can't go. I'll tell
them I don't feel well."
This is a little bit true.

When Jack is worried,
his **tummy** feels funny.

"No!" Billie says. "I
don't want us to miss
out on the hike! We will
have to find something
that looks like Mr. Egg."
She goes into the shed
and looks around for an
idea.

"But what?" says Jack. His tummy is really **hurting** now.

Billie picks up an old soccer ball. Then she finds some rags and wraps them around the ball. Last of all, she finds an old wool hat and squeezes it on top. "Hold this!" she tells Jack.

"I don't know, Billie," he says. "This doesn't look much like Mr. Egg."

"It will in a minute!" says Billie. "Just wait here."

Billie runs back to the house. She returns to the shed in a few minutes. In her hands is the backpack that her parents use to carry her baby brother.

"Look!" says Billie. She takes the soccer ball and puts it in the backpack. Only the wool hat shows at the top. "What do you think?" she says.

"Hmmm ..." says Jack. "It's pretty **silly**. But it just might work!"

Chapter Three

All day, Jack carries the soccer ball in the bag on his back. His parents take lots of photos.

Jack walks quickly so it's hard to see what is really in the backpack.

"Why don't you put Mr. Egg on that rock there?" says Jack's dad. "You and Billie can sit next to him, with Scraps. That would be a great photo."

"Nah!" says Jack. His cheeks turn **pink**. "He looks better in the backpack. Don't you think, Billie?"

"Definitely!" says Billie. They look at each other and try very hard not to laugh.

30

Jack and Billie have a good day. They see lots of birds and a kangaroo.

But on the way home, Jack's tummy starts to hurt again. "What am I going to do tomorrow, Billie?" he whispers. "I can't take an old soccer ball to school instead of Mr. Egg."

"Don't worry," Billie says. "We'll think of something."

Jack smiles. His tummy still hurts. But it hurts less when he shares his worries with Billie.

At home, Jack and Billie help unpack the car. Jack quickly grabs the backpack. But – oh no! The soccer ball **falls out**.

The rags and the hat come off as the ball rolls into the bushes. Scraps runs after it, barking.

"Hey," says his dad. "What's that soccer ball doing in there? And where's Mr. Egg?"

Jack and Billie look at each other. They don't know what to say.

"Scraps!" yells Jack's mom. "Jack, go **catch** your dog. He's run off with that soccer ball. He will put a hole in it!"

Jack and Billie chase Scraps. Scraps chases the ball. He runs into the backyard with it.

Suddenly Jack stops running. He starts laughing instead.

"Billie!" he says.

"I think I know where Mr. Egg is!"

Billie laughs, too.

"Of course!" she says.

"Why didn't we think of that before?"

Billie and Jack arrive
at the end of the
backyard. They see
Scraps **disappear**
behind the woodshed.
There is a narrow gap
between the shed and
the fence. This is where
Scraps hides everything
he steals.

Look! There is Jack's shin guard! And Billie's school hat! There are also lots of balls, including Billie's soccer ball.

Billie and Jack are

happy to find all these

things that have gone

missing. But there is one

thing they are the *most*

happy to see.

Jack pulls Mr. Egg

out from the pile of

treasures.

41

One leg has been chewed, but he is still **smiling**. He seems happy to see them. He is a little bit dirty. But only as dirty as someone who has been on a big adventure!

Read them all!

Hey Jack! The Crazy Cousins
By Sally Rippin

Hey Jack! The Scary Solo
By Sally Rippin

Hey Jack! The Winning Goal
By Sally Rippin

Hey Jack! The Robot Blues
By Sally Rippin

Hey Jack! The Worry Monsters
By Sally Rippin

Hey Jack! The New Friend
By Sally Rippin

Hey Jack! The Worst Sleepover
By Sally Rippin

Hey Jack! The Circus Lesson
By Sally Rippin

Hey Jack! The Bumpy Ride
By Sally Rippin

Hey Jack! The Top Team
By Sally Rippin

Hey Jack! The Playground Problem
By Sally Rippin

Hey Jack! The Best Party Ever
By Sally Rippin

Hey Jack! The Bravest Kid
By Sally Rippin

Hey Jack! The Big Adventure
By Sally Rippin

Hey Jack! The Toy Sale
By Sally Rippin

Hey Jack! The Star of the Week
By Sally Rippin

Hey Jack! The Extra-special Group
By Sally Rippin

Hey Jack! The Other Teacher
By Sally Rippin

Hey Jack! The Party Invite
By Sally Rippin

Hey Jack! The Lost Reindeer
By Sally Rippin

Hey Jack! The Backyard Mystery
By Sally Rippin

Hey Jack! The Special Guest
By Sally Rippin

And don't forget the book starring both Jack and Billie!